Harald "Harry" Shulten
(Mr Harald) (Mr Harry) (Mr H)
(The Garbage Talking Philosopher)
(The CEO of the Dept. of Funny Looks)

Stories from my
Home-Based micro-Business

mrH Enterprises

A Very Expensive Stir

Publisher: Inspiring Publishers,
P.O. Box 159, Calwell, ACT Australia 2905
Email: publishaspg@gmail.com
http://www.inspiringpublishers.com

A catalogue record for this
book is available from the
National Library of Australia

National Library of Australia The Prepublication Data Service

Author: Harald Shulten
Title: Stories from my Home-Based micro-Business
         mrH Enterprises
Genre: Non-fiction
ISBN: 978-1-922792-42-6

ABOUT THIS BOOK & THE AUTHOR

It is now January, 2022 and I am a 68 year old pensioner who lives in Adelaide, South Australia.

Considering all my problems and the way the world is, I have come to realize that there is only one thing that really matters! The free gift of Salvation - the promise of eternal happiness amd eternal peace of mind after I die!
(After I get eaten by maggots) (Ha! Ha!)

So I try and obey the Lord and do things the Bible way. That's why I have included so many scriptures in this book. There are at least a half a dozen Biblical references to everything that has happened or happens in the world. Every sentence, song lyric, or newspaper headline, that was ever spoken or written!

When the Lord asks me (on Judgement Day) to explain myself, I'm just going to hand Him a copy of this book, as well as a copy of my autobiography. (entitled "A Very Expensive Stir") It's the case for my defence!

Just about anyone can start a Home-based micro-Business. All you need is a good idea and a business plan. I've known people who just use their home phone to get customers and then just sub-contract the work out.

I just started out teaching just guitar from home. (in 1982) Then I branched out into other tutoring, research, writing, and consultancy. My first Home based micro-Business was in 1982 and then again in Canberra in 1985.

Attempts that were real disasters.

It should only be 15 minutes of manual book-work at the end of every day to produce a simple Profit & Loss Statement.

God Bless

Harald "Harry" Shulten (Mr Harald) (Mr Harry) (Mr H)
(The Garbage Talking Philosopher)
(The CEO of the Dept. of Funny Looks)

All Glory to the Lord. It is His Will Be Done. He makes the final decision. He has the last say!

FORWARD

Most of my life, I had all sorts of bizarre and degrading problems. Did my problems first start in kindergarten? (c1959) - just after I was molested by a teenage girl. Was all of my life a mixed message, hangman, advertising and media stir? (Doublethink, doublespeak, portmanteau. Is the media playing "Cat & Mouse" with me????)

Who says, writes and does what, where the ideas come from, and who gets paid, cause some massive, bitter and nasty arguments - especially if it involves drugs & alcohol, an invasion of privacy, or a personal attack.

All my problems crashed down on me in Canberra on the night of my birthday in 1985. I didn't know what happened or where I was. It then got worse when I tried to start a home based micro business. I was very unwell for a long time.

Then around the year 2000, I got born again by full immersion in water. I became a born again Christian Fundamentalist and am now able to manage my problems a lot better

Don't Forget to put the Lord First

Seek Ye First the Kingdom of Heaven & His Righteousness & Everything Else Will be Added Unto You (Matt 6:33)

I can Do All Things Through Christ Which Strengthen Me (Phil 4:33)

Be Still and Know that He is God (Ps 46:10)

I Suffer if I Forget to Pray

Now, every night, I bury my sins by confession, remorse, repentance, (think again) and prayer

> Check out these Super-natural Healings!
>
> There are too many to be fraud. Other religeons don't have them.
>
> The Healings don't always happen but they didn't die out with the Apostles. They tell me I'm on the right path!
>
> The Revival Fellowship: The Last Reformation: Curry Blake: Derek Prince: Spirit Filled Churches:

I probably have enough material to write a dozen books and it will keep me busy for the rest of my life.

Probably my next publication will be titled "Bits & Pieces of my Psychosis" followed by my autobiography entitled

"A Very Expensive Stir"

Harald "Harry" Shulten
(Mr Harald) (Mr Harry) (Mr H)
(The Garbage Talking Philosopher)
(The CEO of the Dept. of Funny Looks)

mrH Enterprises
ABN 44 664 504 316
GPO Box 2404
ADELAIDE Sth Australia 5001

© H W Shulten 2021

INDEX

WHAT I DO.

mrH Enterprises is a diverse and creative business that is mainly a Think Tank -With "hands on" knowledge and experience from the "University of Hard Knocks."

mrH does the following

All Types of Research.

Financial, Business, Government, & Legislative Advocacy.

All Types of Training Courses and One-to-One Mentorships.

Music Tuition. (many instruments and styles, mainly guitar) (A baroque, country blues style.)

Private Mini-Corporate Shows and Barbeques. I play an un-amplified, solo, accoustic guitar.

Unique Sessions on Politics, Religeon & the Media.

Thousands of fascinating stories from my autobiography "A Very Expensive Stir."

New Approaches, Concepts, & Ideas are almost guranteed.

Low Cost, Negotiable Fees.

mrH is based on Born Again Christian Components.

The best way to contact or approach me is in writing.
GPO Box 2404 Adelaide Sth Australia 5001
harrysummersea@yahoo.com.au

WHERE DO I GET MY IDEAS FROM?

SNOW-FLAKING (Brain-storming)

- I would rather get my ideas from the Bible. The Lord knows and owns everything. To Him, "there is nothing new under the sun" (Eccl 1:9) A mortal man however, has relatively limited intelligence, and in his limited frame of reference, he can always find something new.
- I would rather not get my ideas from other people.
- I don't like sneaking up behind other people and stealing the words out of their mouths. (as was done to me)

The Snowflake Structure & Format of Mathematics, a Financial Statement, Precise, Synopsis, or other Summary

Consider a simple black and white diagram or photo of a snowflake.

You can use the same design, geometry, layout and format to present Maths, a Financial Statement, Precise, Synopsis or other Summary.

It is aesthetically pleasing, easy to look at, and easy to understand.

Also "Snowflaking" is a word I use instead of "brainstorming"

In brainstorming, you use a nucleus of a word or idea, draw a bubble around it, then extrapolate with arrows - forming other bubbles, words, and ideas.

The Lord uses the nucleus of a water molecule to produce the infinitely unique designs and geometry of a snowflake. No two snowflakes are the same.

It is interesting because man made artificial snow doesn't have the intricate crystalline structure.

(Job 38: 22-28) "Hast Thou Considered the Treasures of the Snow?"

How did the writer know, centuries before the invention of the microscope, that every snowflake was a uniquely, ornamented, carved piece of geometric jewelry? They are all different.

It's interesting to note that the man-made, artificial snow, doesn't have the unique designs and crystalline structure

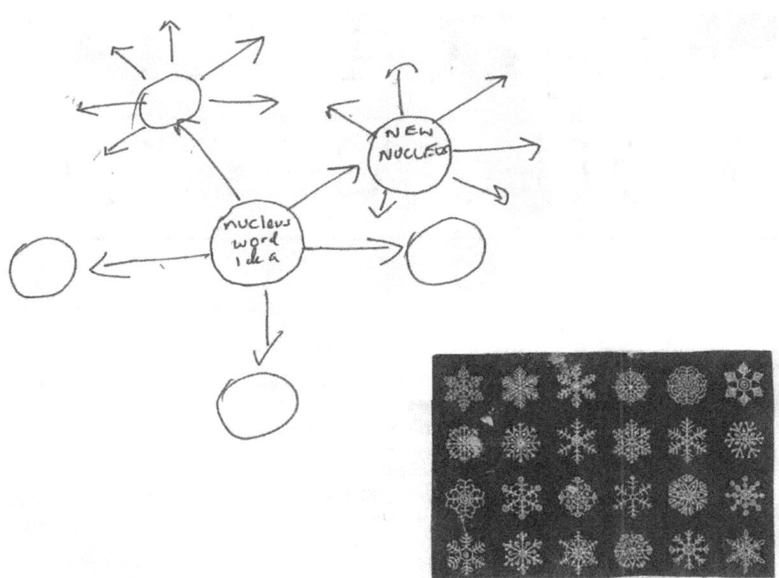

THE BEST RESEARCH PROJECT THAT YOU CAN GET

The Best Research Project that You Can Get

In the 1960's, as a youngster in Primary School, my main childhood heroes were Jesus, The Absent-minded Professor, the Marx Brothers, and Bugs Bunny - (in that order)

I always wanted to be like the Absent-minded Professor and be the first to discover something new – something as good as "Flubber" (flying rubber) The formula for Flubber was the same as the formula for success.

My last year in school was Matriculation (Year 12, in 1970). It took me 15 years to realize that I was victimised by a group of individuals in the SA Education Dept. All my results were under-graded and outright wrong – to the point of failing. School was a massive, wasted work effort that made me ill.

Never the less, in 1971, I managed to get to University and was looking forward to a relatively easy life as a researcher, mathematician or school teacher. Unfortunately, after many bizarre and degrading incidents, my university science career messed up badly. I didn't know that it messed up big time. Mixed message, head-stuff, hangman, newspaper articles should have told me so! Articles like the "psychologist broken nose" and "pet rock" stories should have told me so! Also, the "Dark Glasses" story

After a poor attempt at addressing my problems, I locked myself away in my room with a blind obsession of becoming a better guitar player. What a mistake! Never again! – but that's another story!

I was overcome with nervousness, anxiety and depression. **I was looking for a happy place to escape to**. Everything was useless because it withers and dies and then gets eaten by maggots. (Ha! Ha!) Absolutely everything! At the time I didn't worship the Lord and didn't realize that the only thing that really matters is the free gift of Salvation – the promise of eternal happiness and peace of mind after you die.

Then around the year 2000, I got witnessed to and became a Born Again Christian Fundamentalist. The Bible has many fascinating scientific verses.

A merry heart doeth good like a medicine but a broken spirit drieth the bones (Prov. 17:22)

This suggests that in a depressed person, the blood cells don't form properly and that he hasn't got a good oxygen intake. A naturopath once told me that the secret to happiness is "one hour's good oxygen uptake a day" You won't get this in a city. You need to go to a large, open, oxygen rich, place like the country, beach, a park, or a forest.

Biblical Food Laws (Lev. 11:3)

Most religions have similar food laws – vegetables, grain, fish, nuts, honey, etc. It implies that they all have the same origin. There are no food laws in the New Testament (the New Agreement) The Bible only says to put healthy food in your body and treat it like a temple. In the Old Testament however, certain foods were forbidden depending on offal, cloven hooves, no fins and no scales. It suggests that if the biochemists studied the genetic linkages of this, then they might have a different insight as to why a cell becomes diseased or cancerous.

Then in 2018, I was listening to the CHIPS Diet program on Seventh Day Adventist radio (Radio 3ABN) The presenters said that non-scale sea animals like oysters, prawns, octopus, and crabs, don't filter their waste properly. They also said that cancer cells need a compound called "methionine" to grow and normal, healthy cells don't. Methionine is a compound mostly found in offal and animal waste. The program said that the race was on between the biochemists to find out how to neutralize it. It seems to me that the Bible is telling us where to look for a cure for cancer. The implication is that disease, cancer and sickness originate in animal waste. How I wish I had read that when I was a university biochemistry student in the early 70's.

In the Bible Numerics, the number 6 is usually associated with Satan. It has common letters and sounds with the words sin, sick, sex and shit. Do they all have the same origin?

Fasting (many scriptures - refer Strom's Bible Concordance)

The Bible also says a lot about fasting and many people are healed during a prayer and fast. There was a lot of interest in fasting from around 2015 and one Australian Weight Loss company adopted it – the first change it had made in 30 years. In 2019, two North - American researchers won the Nobel Prize for the research they did into fasting. Why should they get the Nobel Prize for something that was written in the Bible 2000 years ago? It seems to me that the Nobel Prize should go to the Lord.

....

Anyway, there are many fascinating scientific research scriptures whereby the Lord proves His own existence and superior intelligence and energy.

e.g.

the "paths of the seas" (ocean currents) (Psalm 8:8)

"the treasures of the snow" (Job 38:22)

"the water cycle" (Eccl 1:7)

"the Great Pyramid at Giza" (Isaiah 19:19)

The Bible is the best research project you can get.

It's also free and you don't need a grant.

Check out the supernatural healings on the following Born again Christian Fundamentalist Websites

The Healings don't always happen but they didn't die out with the Apostles. There are too many of them to be fraud. The other religions don't have them. They tell me I'm on the right path.

The Revival Fellowship: The Last Reformation: Curry Blake: Derek Prince: Spirit Filled Churches

HAPPY MATHEMATICS FOR STRUGGLING BATTLERS

Have you ever struggled with any form of maths? - to the point of being anxious, visibly agitated, completely turned off, and destroyed? Then this is for you!

Happy Mathematics for Struggling Battlers

I had a lot of problems (as a teenager) at Salisbury High School, (1966 -1970) They later got worse when I worked for the SA Education Dept.- e.g. the media and advertising lackeys were no good. The bigger kids also bullied, and often thumped my younger brother and I. Years later I felt guilty, because I took it out on him.

Years later an ex-student and one of our country general store customer's told me "the whole school was no good! All the bodgies & widgies came from miles around to go there. I'm leaving the area before this all blows up in their faces"

On the surface, I was a cheeky, arrogant, smart aleck, but underneath things got to me. In those days, I had a double gold filling in my two front teeth and was sometimes called "a rat with a gold tooth"

Never-the-less, in the 60's, Salisbury High was drug and alcohol free. I had some really good teachers and was always grateful for being given a solid grounding & base in the three "R's"

In 1966, our Year 8 class was chosen to be the guinea pigs for the so called "New Maths" - some of which was taught at university. It turned a lot of students off for-ever, but I myself, thrived on it. For the next three years we had a really good teacher (Mr K.S.) He applied everything, gave freely of his knowledge, and spontaneously rattled everything off the top of his head.

He gave me my nickname of "Harry"

He once apologised for setting a test that was way too hard and told the class "I'll never forget the look that Harry gave me!"

I was fascinated by a book called "Riddles in Mathematics" Once I got excited when I devised a different little geometrical notation that proved that one equals two. I thought the Education Dept would pay me a lot of money to re-structure everything. Need-less to say, Mr K.S. ripped my stupid logic apart in two seconds flat - so it was back to the drawing board

After three years, Mr K.S. was given a senior transfer to Marryattville High School – the first music focused school in the state. The first school to teach the rock, pop, blues and jazz music. A well known local and national rock musician was also given a job there. He couldn't handle what the music business did to him (or do I mean musical fraud?) he lodged a complaint because his wages were always wrong and I got told that it caused a lot of suspicion.

When I left school, I wanted to be a maths teacher or researcher but everything messed up. (badly)

I didn't realize that I was targeted by a section of the Education Dept. and all my exam results were outright under-graded and wrong - to the point of failure. Mixed message newspaper articles should have also told me that it messed up big time. Stories like the "Pet Rock" and "Psychologist Broken Nose" articles. Also the "The Dark Glasses" So, I dropped out of Uni in 1974. I never knew what hit me nor where I was.

I was completely overwhelmed with stress, depression and anxiety. Instead of facing up to my problems, I would lock myself away in my room with a blind obsession of becoming a better guitar player - but that's another story. What a mistake! Never again!

I was looking for a happy place to escape to, Now 47 years later, in 2021, I sometimes have a re-kindled desire to tutor Maths. How am I going to do that when my knowledge is so out of date? I'll need to apply and adapt all the maths that I remember in my 50 year working life in budgets, finance and business. Surely, I can still teach year 11 Maths!

So here are some interesting Applied Maths Stories

<u>No.1</u> Around 2014, I went to a lecture by a world acclaimed Flinders Uni Maths Professor - just to see how much I could remember. It was held at the Adelaide Town Hall and was open to the general public. It was instant suspicion as soon as I walked in. The foyer was like a morgue and all these people were looking at me. There was a rapid exchange of funny looks and quite a few people stared daggers. These people should adjust their facial expressions to reflect sympathetic encouragement. The lecture ended with a classical music recital and the associated booklet was exactly the same as one that I myself had previously produced.

During the lecture, a lot instantly came back to me and I could follow most of the talk.

One of the questions asked was "is God playing dice with the universe?" The Bible answers that question.

It mentions worldly numerology - that the numbers in the physical or natural world make certain patterns, but be wary of it. You will not understand. Then there is the Biblical

Mathematical Seal or Bible Numerics. Biblical and spiritual numbers make even more complicated patterns than the worldly numerology and no computer has ever been able to do the same.

No.2 When I first learned about the history of ancient Egypt, (at school) all the good stuff was left out. The geometry and mathematics of the Great Pyramid at Gizah, are fascinating. It's the same maths as in the Bible. "there in the midst of Egypt, and the borders there of, stands a testimony in stone (to the Lord)" (Isaiah 19:19)

No.3 In 1971, I had a uni friend who was a maths and physics whizz. He told me that if you fired a gun, you could mathematically prove that the bullet hits the target before you pull the trigger. At the time, I thought "what sort of a stupid calculation is that?" However, it tells me that the three different time zones, (the past, present & future), all co-exist together. "Jesus Christ, the same yesterday, today, & tomorrow) (Heb 13:8) The Lord has a different concept of time and can move freely in between all three. "His ways are not our ways" (Isa 55:8)

No. 4 I once went to a physics lecture and my head was already stuffed. Absolutely great????

Then I realized that it was only a single page of basic year 12 maths to produce the simple formula of $E = mc^2$ If you can't do the easy stuff and produce a simple empirical formula nothing else will work.

No. 5 I was a part time, after hours, guitar teacher for 30 years and always lacked some basic listening and comprehension skills - as did a lot of my students. I had a lot more success when I taught the background mathematics, geometry and science of music. It took me 50 years (part time) to structure a very simple Grade 5 Course. An eight year old, would learn it all in seven years - half an hour a day, providing they were happy and had a sense of getting better.

While I was teaching, some people snuck up behind me and stole the words out of my mouth. I ended up completely miserable because I gave away all my Intellectual Property for nothing. Most of my students were quite decent and O.K., but how many leeches suck the blood out of a stone?

<u>No. 6</u> A pensioner once told me that one of the greatest lessons you can learn in life is, at the end of every day, write down everything you have spent. Do the simple sums. Even Albert Einstein did that.

I may only have a low turn-over, Home Based Micro-Business, but it only takes me 10 minutes, every evening, to manually do all my book work.

<u>No. 7</u> In the 1800's, money didn't turn over as fast as it does today. People often only paid a debt once a year. It's still a problem - especially in small country towns - although I get told the situation has improved over the last 20 years.

There is a very low profit margin in groceries and a 25% mark-up means a 20% profit (compared to retail prices) Half of this is lost in freight, electricity and theft. So generally speaking, a shop-keeper **has a 10% pre-tax income. If a customer only pays his account every three months, it's a lot of intermittent background work, over a long time - for just a few hours wages.**

When my parents owned their deli's, we should have had a Budget Advice Service. (BAS) We should have trimmed our customers' household, business and farming costs. It would have been the same as free groceries. The same as giving them the money to shop with us! Monthly, cost-cutting, social evenings would also benefit a small community. Why did it take me over 30 years of living in the past to think of this???? A teacher at high school called the students "Numb-skulls!"

No. 8 If you think being an accountant is a boring job, try sorting out a fraud problem. The perpetrators have to do a lot else wrong to cover their tracks and the paper trail. The associated confusion, degrading sexism, often violent abuse and racism, are something to behold. To avoid being ripped off is a good reason to learn maths.

No. 9 The media is full of bull-sh*t numbers and mixed messages. Usually confusion like that is an indication of fraud. Does the media fuel a fire and perpetuate a stir with hangman, mixed messages???? Is there such a thing as "Mixed Message, Hangman, Character Assasination????" The media is a completely ruthless and cut-throat, two faced, mixed message, hangman stir. Does the media play "Cat & Mouse????"

No. 10 In the Old Testament there was only simple interest and all debts had to be wiped out clean after seven years. If a loan went bad, then the lender lost his money - not the borrower. In the early 1900's the banks realized that they could make a lot more money by charging compound interest and stretching the loan over 20 or 30years. They make you pay most of the interest first - before you repay the principal of the loan.

No. 11 The GST proved to be financial windfall and the country should have money coming out of its ears. Instead we've got a massive national debt. Also, the background reasoning given for all the Economic Stimulus Packages doesn't make good mathematical sense.

No. 12 The individual financial steps and background logic of how slaves were bought and sold in Biblical times, make a fascinating story. So too is how Christ set the captives free by paying for our sins and debt with His suffering, blood and sacrificial death. A debt that we couldn't pay. (The Redemption & Resurrection)

The Bible tells you to avoid debt "You are a slave to the lender" (Prov 22:7)

Many of us live on credit and all the figures are disappearing into cyber space. Computers are great when they work but useless broken toys, if they are hacked, or if there is a power failure. All the world's finances, communications, travel, and weapons systems, are balanced, and hinged, on a broken toy.

No.13 I've seen many shop assistants that can't do basic sums and calculate change. It's mostly a matter of $a - b = c$ or $a = b + c$ or $xa + xb = x(a+b)$

No.14 I think Australia put a curse on itself when Valentine's Day (14/2/66) was chosen as the Decimal Currency change-over date. Are people supposed to love each other with money and laugh it off as a joke? Choosing the first day of the New Financial Year would have been more logical. By freak coincidence, the advertising jingle (sung to the tune of Click Go the Shears) was the first or second song my brother and I ever played in public (on our guitars)

No.15 If the basic mathematics of any matter isn't correct and done in good faith, then you have sown a bad seed. It will explode out of all proportion - especially a financial transaction. (Gal 6: 7-9) "What you sow, is what you reap"

Check out the Healings on these Born Again, Christian Fundamentalist sites:

The Healings don't always happen but they didn't die out with the Apostles.

Other Religeons don't have them. They tell me that I am on the right path.

The Revival Fellowship: The Pioneer School: Curry Blake: Derek Prince: Spirit Filled Churches.

THE FARCE OF EVOLUTION

**There are many problems with Darwin's Theory
of Evolution**

Problem No.1 The Chicken and the Egg

Which came first? The answer is that the rooster, chicken and egg can't instantaneously evolve from each other from nothing. There are no fossils that show any gradual evolutionary change. All three have to appear on the planet at the same time. – i.e. God made them all at the same time.

Problem No.2 Intelligent Design

Some scientists won't use the word "God" and prefer the term "Intelligent Design"

The example sometimes given is a mouse trap. Someone has to think of the original idea. Then they have to make the individual parts because they're all different and can't all instantly evolve from each other out of nothing. Then someone has to put it all together, place the cheese and make it work.

Problem No.3 The Lung Fish

Some scientists say the first land animals were the lung fish which crawled out of the ocean. They claim all other land animals evolved from them. If that's the case there should be many millions of fossils showing the gradual change. There is not one.

Problem No.4 The Missing Link

In the 70's, my biology tutor told me that scientists had reasoned that there was no such thing as the "missing link" in the evolution of man from the apes. The modern-day ape and humans both evolved independently from a common ancestor. I think it was considered a major breakthrough in scientific thinking. However, it wasn't even a drop in the ocean.

Problem No.5

I get told that apes have 95% of the same genetic make up as a human. It doesn't mean they both evolved from a common ancestor. The Bible says that God made all animals separately and according to their own kind. So too will they reproduce (Gen 1:24)

Problem No.6 The Second Law of Thermo-Dynamics

This states that if you place an object in a given space, then given enough time, it will eventually disintegrate- so that all the individual atoms spread evenly through-out that space. The only process in the universe which contradicts this, is the energy form called "life"

Problem No.7 The Sub- Atomic Structure & the God Particle.

After Einstein worked out the sub-atomic structure, he realized that there was nothing holding it together. He reasoned that this was the Spirit of God and became a Christian. I think in the 90's, scientists found a way of measuring the energy that holds the sub atomic particles together, and called it the "God Particle"

Problem No.8 Amino Acids

If life created itself at random from nothing, what's the chance of all amino acids being left handed molecules?

Problem No.9 The Fruit Fly.

Scientists have made genetic changes to the fruit fly which are equivalent to millions of years of evolution. It's still a fruit fly.

Problem No.10 Blood

I get told the salt concentration of human blood is the same as sea water. It doesn't mean that man evolved from the lung fish. If God had the ability to create Adam from the dust of the earth, He had the ability to make blood from sea water.

Problem No.11 Food Laws

Most religions tell you to eat the same foods – i.e. Fruit, vegetables, grains, honey, nuts, etc. It implies that all religions had a common origin and, that in the very beginning, the Lord told people what to eat.

There are no food laws in the New Testament but in the Old Testament certain foods were forbidden – based on whether the animal had un-cloven hooves, scales or ate offal. If the biochemists researched the genetic linkages of this, they might get another insight as to why a cell becomes diseased or cancerous.

Problem No. 12 Who made God?

At uni in the 70's one lecturer claimed that if you say God created life, then you still have the same problem. You have to ask yourself "Who made God?" The Bible answers that question. It clearly says that no mortal man was given the intelligence to understand that. WE will never understand who made God, infinity, the creation of the universe, or the Lord's superior time frame. "God's ways are not our ways" (Isaiah 55:8)

How was the Universe created? The Bible supports the "Big Bang Theory"

"In the beginning was the Word" (John 1:1) I gather this means there was only the Spirit of God in the form of sound. Then God said "Let there be Light" (Gen1:3) I gather He converted sound into light. Then he made the firmament and then living things. (see Genesis) I think scientists say that sound, light and matter are all inter-convertible! To me there is nothing remarkable about the "Big Bang Theory"

The Bible tells me that it is possible that the God created the universe out of nothing after an explosion.

Problem No.13 Seven Days

Scientists often ask – "how can anyone produce such a complex universe in seven days?" The word "day' comes from the ancient Hebrew word "yon" which means "a period of time" Also the Bibles says that, in the Lord's time frame, a day is the same as a week, the same as a thousand years which means a second is the same as a million years. The Lord made the universes in seven periods of time and it doesn't say all the periods were all equal.

Problem No.14

There must be many thousands of books published about biochemistry, genetics, evolution and the origins of life.

Mortal man still can't even understand the basics of the energy form that is life. WE haven't even solved a speck of dust in the universe. The Extent of the complicated nature implies the existence of a superior God. The complexity of the physical or natural world. How the billions of different micro systems fit together and interact to survive. "The mere fact that creation exists is enough proof" (Rom: 1:20)

Problem No.15

Many people, including scientists, boast about their superior worldly intelligence. They boast about their competent, worldly, problem solving skills. What did Jesus say on the cross when the ignorant masses persecuted Him with their worldly knowledge, logic and reasoning? "Forgive them Father. They know not what they do"

> **You really need to have a one to one experience with the Lord to really believe that He, and only He, created the world and the universe.**

The easiest way to have such a one to one experience is to go outside on a starry night. You are looking right at Him. You can feel the presence of a superior energy form and intelligence.

You can also ask Him for a sign or to prove that He exists. See what happens.

Also, The Bible has many inbuilt proofs where-by the Lord proves his own existence. For example:

The Bible Numerics (The mathematical seal that the Lord put on the Bible via the ancient Hebrew and ancient Greek languages) Refer the work of Ivan Panin.

The Great Pyramid at Gizah (It's design, mathematics and geometry) (Isaiah 19:19)

The Aswan Dam (Ezekial 30:12)

The Treasures of the Snow (Job 38:22)

The Description of the Water Cycle - centuries before mortal man discovered it (Job 26:8) (Job 28:26) (Job 36:27) (Job 38:33)

95% of Bible Prophecies have come true (Refer mostly Daniel & Revelations)

Jesus still heals today. The super-natural healings didn't die out with the Apostles.

The List of Proofs goes on

MR HARRY'S SCHOOL OF APPLIED GUITAR

Recommended (mostly) for Adults Only

<u>Mr Harald (Mr Harry)</u> Basic Musical Tips for Amateurs or Happy Idiots like Me

Stories from Mr Harald's School of Applied Guitar

I always wanted an easy life as a school teacher, researcher, or mathematician. In the early 70's, however, after many bizarre and degrading incidents, my university science career messed up. I didn't realize that it was big time. Mixed message, hangman, newspaper articles like the "pet rock" and "psychologist broken nose" stories should have told me so. Also "The Dark Glasses"

Who wants an education? I'm better off just being a happy idiot! **One doctor told me that my biggest talent was helping people with depression. Another doctor told me that people were interested in my ability with words.** He didn't explain what he meant and I couldn't remember what he said for decades. Do I really want to be associated with what mortal man does in the name of intelligence? An "insult" to the superior "intelligence" of a happy idiot!

I couldn't face up & made a poor attempt at addressing my problems.So I locked myself away in my room with a blind obsession to become a better guitar player. Regrettably, some housemates were probably driven nuts. What a mistake! Never Again!

I was a miserable guitar player, who locked himself away in his room. I was looking for a happy place to escape to. It took me decades to realize, that the only happy place worth escaping to, is the peace and rest of the Lord.

I was completely destroyed by anxiety, depression, and stress. At the time, I didn't worship the Lord and didn't know about His blessings. Everything in the physical or natural world was useless because it withers and dies. I knew not that the only thing that really matters is the free gift of Salvation (i.e. eternal happiness and eternal peace of mind after my body gets eaten by maggots) Ha! Ha!

(see the Book of Ecclesiastes – the philosophers' explanation of the Scriptures)

<u>Music & Kaizen</u>

Music was always a confusing and frustrating head-stuff. I literally spent decades (after hours, part time) working out what to do with a one foot arm movement & a one inch finger movement. I could only understand some of the concepts. It took me decades to apply my knowledge, produce the goods, and make things happen. I sometimes look at music as "Opal Mining" I spent years chipping away at the frustrating, confusing and worthless potch -just so I could have some awakening moments of discovery and find a few buried gem stones

I had to do music bit by bit – structure and piece it together in bits and pieces.

Kaizen is Japanese word meaning "over a period of time, a lot of small, incremental, daily life changes in an individual or community, eventually add up to a massive result". It is how many countries rebuilt their entire infrastructure after the devastation of WW2

I got a new lease of life when I focused on the Gospel music. So what do the Biblical scriptures say about Kaizen? "What you sow is what you reap" (Gal 6: 7-9) "From a tiny seed a mighty mustard tree grows" (Mark 4: 30-32) What are the healing, building and structural properties of a plant like mustard?

I think there is a Kaizen Institute in Japan and the concept can be applied to almost any problem

I think that the Education system has come to realize that the happy experiences a person has in the first 3 or 4 years of life, determine their abilities, skills, and talent, as an adult (including reading your child bedtime stories and playing him music)

In 1964, when we were 10 and 11, my parents bought my brother and I, a guitar each. They wanted us to be able to play music at a party. We, however, were more interested in reading our MAD comics. WE imitated the antics of the "Three Stooges" - so our parents banned us from watching the show. Instead, we had to do our guitar practice

Our first teacher was an orchestra leader, and unbelievably, in 7 years, we never heard him play guitar once. It took a whole year before we could play our first tune and we couldn't understand why he didn't explain anything. Then decades later I realized that he didn't want to give away his Intellectual Property. He made us work.

By contrast I've had other teachers who freely handed me all their knowledge on a silver platter – e.g. a Tae Kwon Do Instructor who was also a professional musician.

One of the few song books available at the time was "The Ukulele Songbook" Now a days, 55 years later, there is an infinite amount of learning material available. How Rock and Pop music has evolved! (in so many different ways!) Kids these days sure have got it a lot easier.

After 7 years my brother and I could play rhythm guitar and read music, but couldn't do much else. Not many youngsters could play guitar like us in those days - but now-a-days we wouldn't be looked at.

WE were too young to understand that if the teacher gave us some sheet music we were supposed to pay for it. We sometimes stirred him up, but he and his wife were completely decent, and treated us like kings

- I loved it when a dance teacher told me "music is like pizza! The most important part is the base (Bass) – everything else is topping!" My contribution to that, is that the tomato sauce and cheese are the middle voices. On the surface, this sounds a bit stupid, but what it says is, that some people only listen to the overall sound of a piece of music – i.e. the bigger picture. If you empathize and break the sound up into low, middle, and top parts, it's easier to recognize and remember the individual musical steps.

- I always lacked some basic listening skills and had to do a lot of music by maths. In 1968, at the age of 15, the first tune I could play by ear was the "Marlboro Man" (The Magnificent Seven) A year later another cigarette ad appeared which featured my Christian name of Harald (Harold???) WE ridiculed the ad by imitation and role play and lit up with a Marlboro. IN other words, I started smoking for a joke. The initial taste was that bad that I never thought I would get hooked, but I have had a chronic problem for 47 years. Satan is very good at back firing a joke – especially with drugs and alcohol! **Was all my life an advertising & media stir? – starting in kindergarten (c1958)? – just after I got molested by a teenage girl?**

IN 1977, when I was 23, my parents bought a small country town Grocery and General Store. Despite having no experience, I was asked to teach guitar at the local primary school. There was no one else. A Hal Leonard guitar manual suggested teaching one finger, one chord songs to beginners. I put a lot of my own time and work into that. The next thing I knew, someone in the Education Dept got some career mileage by producing a whole booklet of one chord songs

I couldn't understand why one youngster couldn't tell the difference between a line and a space nor understand the letters E, F & G. Then I realized that as a seven year old, he hadn't learned the letters of the alphabet His mother told me that since he had been doing music, his reading and writing had dramatically improved. Later I found out that he became a school teacher

- Years later I saw one child on TV claim he didn't realize that he had to "read the black stuff" Years later, at an art course, I learned about positive and negative shapes and how different people can see different things on a page. Memorizing shapes & pictures is one way of learning. Years later, I realized that it was just as important to learn how to write music at the same time as learning to read it.

- My guitar class only learned for three months, and then did a school concert item. A few parents told me "I didn't know my child had the ability to do that!" It was only a matter of being given the opportunity and being shown how. Every musician starts off by being shown how. They only think for themselves much later on.

In 1982, I had a working holiday in Queensland. The tourism ads, with all the beautiful girls on the beautiful beaches, put this stupid idea in my head that only happy people lived there. I met a Maori who was a really good natural player. He could instantly work out and play complicated four voice, jazz tunes by ear. I always find that the most natural players are the Maoris and some of the other South Pacific Islanders. Most of them can play without really being shown how. Their ancestors all originated from South America and their natural ability probably stems from the sounds and rhythms they listen to in their culture. The Maori bands had female lead guitarists decades before any-one else did!

The Maori I met wanted to learn how to read music and I couldn't understand why he was unable to distinguish between the letters E, F and G. Then, when he miss-read and confused the sheet music to "Yakkety Sax" with "Yesterday", I realized that he couldn't read or write. How did he ever get through school without the teachers noticing? By freak chance, I found out that a couple of years later, the 60 Minutes Show did a negative story on the NZ education system. The reporter asked the same thing – i.e. "How did he get through school without the teachers noticing?" Am I going nuts here or what? Over the years I had many problems with what was shown on television. Is this believable? Am I going nuts here or what?

In 1995, I had a student successes story with an intellectually disadvantaged nine year old. No one would teach him - but I became interested in his disability. I wanted to do something new and different. He had the abilities of a five year old and teaching him was sheer agony. He would never be another Elvis.

I should have always given him a glass of water to settle his breathing, make sure his mouth wasn't dry, and make sure he wasn't dehydrated. Years later, a naturo-path told me that chewing on a raisin, without swallowing, exercises the jaw and stimulates blood flow and saliva production.

I taught him at his own pace and tried to simplify music, using words that he could understand. I painstakingly broke up and simplified the rhythms I was showing him. I encouraged him to "scat" play and make the sounds that he could. I tidied up a song that I showed him how to write and he sang it for his church group – speech impediment and all.

Years later I thought a good exercise for him would have been to make sounds like "da, da," to the two note music of the film "Jaws" (Shark Attack) Another good tune for him would have been the two note bass line to "Walk on the Wild Side"

Playing a recorder, tin whistle, harmonica or any wind instrument would also have been good for him. He'll never be a professional musician, but after four agonizing years, he could play a good basic guitar.

His problem was complicated. I got paid, so hopefully, I helped him properly. (How many times did I get worked over with the word "help?") His mother later told me that his disability diagnosis got re-assessed to that of just being a slow learner.

> A few years later, I met a disability worker who showed me one of her government manual's. I recognized some of the content as the work I had done with my students. The disability worker just sneered at the manual and said that she had to go to the toilet. I've also met people who told me that their employer pays thousands of dollars to external consultants to conduct training courses and the staff just go to the toilet.
>
> It was completely suspicious and I can't explain why I didn't ask her about it. Later, I also became suspicious about the behind-the-scenes production and politics of Adelaide produced disability films like "Shine" and "The King's Speech"

- Later, as a born again Christian Fundamentalist, I found a Biblical Scripture that said "we are all born with sound minds" It implies everyone has some sort of musical ability The Lord also does a lot with sound and does a lot with very little.

<u>Learning to Sing</u> I could sing at school and always got into the school or church choir. That was before my voice cracked because of the cigarettes. I sometimes went to singing lessons and was made to sing sounds like "Mee, aw, ah" to specific notes. I now realize that an amateur doesn't need that. He only needs to experiment and find his natural voice – i.e. just make the sounds that he can. Just match your voice to the resonance of the chords or music! For an amateur, singing is just like talking! Only a professional needs to train his voice – like an "athlete training his body." Some singing teachers say that it all depends on your diction and how you shape the words in your mouth. Many jazz musicians look at their musical instrument as an extension of their voice. Even the instrumental music comes out of their mouths!

What Makes a Good Student or a Successful Person?

They start young. They're genuinely happy to spend a long time doing what they do – without the untrustworthy glossed over positive energy. They're always rested and never study or practice - they only research! They are always looking for an answer! Many of them also get paid or are already rich

---

Was I the First Guitar Player in the World to Play a Baroque Country Blues Style?

Am I talking garbage? I always wanted to find something new. I like to decorate all my notes differently - like snowflakes, crystals or diamonds. (When I play, I scatter handfuls of unpolished gem stones I produce little blobs of sound or energy How do you convert the Lord's infinite imagination, shapes and designs into sound? Again, am I talking garbage? I can't really tell.

Is MUSIC Really Worth it? Music was always one bizarre and degrading incident after another for me. It cost me a lot of money. People snuck up behind me and stole the words out of my mouth. I had a lot of Intellectual Property problems and call the music business "Musical Fraud" I get a carrot dangled in front of me and get treated like a donkey. How many leeches suck the blood out of a stone? There must also have been something major wrong with the way I got set up alone with some women and children. Was I shown some dodgy fraudulent videos? I had many problems with what they put on TV. Did I see that right?

I got comments like "Talk about a country shooting itself in the foot because it forgets about the money!" Useless generalizations like "All Australians are bas*****s!" "Stars have to be helped" and "too far to go" stories "My mother wants me to be a rock star and she bashes me" "An individual had a whole body of work stolen from him" "It sucks"

- Some people (not all) are gold digging leeches. They suck the blood out of a stone and claim they are helping you. Then they stuff their faces at a very expensive restaurant, knock off $100 bottles of red wine or champagne and can't contain themselves laughing.
- I never really worked again since I either left or got kicked out of the Public Service in 1994. In 2018, I've been actively pitching what I write and do for 24 years. I almost never get a reply- let alone a decent work offer. I once pitched my music at a film producer and he said it was "nice music but it's only average" which became the album title of my first CD. At least he didn't try and pump me up to sell me a dodgy record contract. Whenever I ask people "what are you paying to do what?" they all shut up real quick!

Never-the-less, **After 55 years**, I met many decent people. I got a new lease of life when I got witnessed to, got born again, and started playing the Gospel Music. It took me 55 years to structure a very simple and easy to understand Grade 5 level music course. An 8 year old would learn it all in 7 years - half an hour a day providing they were happy and had a sense of getting better. At the age of 65, I have a nice little part time income from a home based micro business. It gives me something to do. **Sometimes I'm happy!** At 65, I'd like to be well paid for writing one classic before I die - before my body gets eaten by maggots. (Ha! Ha!)

GROCERY SHOPPING MONEY SAVERS

Grocery Shopping Money Savers

A lot of marketing and psychological research goes into maximising supermarket sales.

Essential items like milk, bread, meat, are usually placed at the back of the store to make a customer walk past all the other goods first.

Wholesalers pay the supermarkets a kick-back to display their products at eye level.

When entering a store most people walk to the right and walking clock-wise or anti-clockwise also affects how much they spend. On the surface these marketing and psychological strategies seem a bit stupid but they work!

TIPS

If you don't have a debt, you don't need any money. Generally speaking, if you don't spend the money, you don't have to work for it. How do the sayings go? "A penny saved is a penny earned" and "take care of the pennies and the pounds will take care of themselves"

Shop relaxed, in a good mood, and take time. Don't go shopping when you're hungry. Eat first. Also, if you go shopping in a bad mood, it's likely to get worse. Also, if you're in a bad mood and don't know what to do for a meal, there's more chance you will buy a more expensive take-a-way. Have a rest instead.

Know the prices before hand and make a list and budget. Stick to it! Only take the amount of money you need – take cash and no ATM card

Work out the unit cost of each item – e.g. the price per 100 gms.

Take an extra $5 or $10 and buy non – perishable specials to stock pile (e.g. rice, pasta, canned goods, etc.) Shop at the end of the day or week-end when prices are reduced

Buy generic brands. Buy left-over meat pieces. Use cheaper cuts of meat in stews and casseroles

Buy in season fruit and veg. You can make many cheap and simple two ingredient meals – even if you can't cook.

Glossy packaged cleaning products are expensive. Clean with natural products like vinegar, bi-carb and lemons. All the "know - how" is on the internet.

Pies, pasties and soft drinks are a lot cheaper in a supermarket than a take-a-way shop

Beware of "impulse buys" That's why supermarkets put lollies and chocolates on the counter next to the cash register.

Barter with your neighbours if they have fruit trees, a vegetable garden, or other goods.

Local community markets are usually cheaper than the bigger supermarkets. Organic too!

If you personally know the owner of an independent store, become a regular customer and try and barter for a better deal

Write your own cook book listing all your own cheap meals. Pre- Prepare your meals and shop in advance.

Build up a support group. The best way is to build up your own little Christian fellowship and worship at home or outdoors. Jesus spent very little time in a temple or church building.

Would You Like to Own a Little Shop?

In the 70's and 80's, my parents, brother and I, worked hundreds of 12 to 16 hour days in our two deli's and small country town general store. What a completely wasted work effort! The big profits aren't there in groceries.

Your business is also your home and it was like having several hundred people in your lounge room every day. (seven days a week)

It busted us and was partially responsible for wrecking my university science research career.

We thought all we had to do was run an honest business that sold good quality goods as cheaply as we could. How wrong we were! All those never- ending, degrading arguments about money – every day! For over nine years! WE got used to them and thought it was normal to have arguments like that. Some customers loved to start an internal argument – especially between the two big brothers.

WE must also have copped it every time there were television advertising specials with a focus on "sex sells"

On the surface, I carried on like a cheeky smart aleck, but underneath things got to me. I was sometimes called a "rat with a gold tooth"

I'll remember the first time we got accused of cheating. In 1971, a bread roll cost four cents and we copped a vitriolic comment of "these two young boys with their beautiful eyes are nothing but cheats – just like their parents"

WE always had a core group of loyal customers who wouldn't shop any-where else (a niche market) Other people, however, gave us a nasty time and a complete working over. That's before I start talking about the physically violent threats. They were still the days before Australia had a major drug and alcohol problem.

Over the years I became aware of the dis-proportionate number of deli owners and other small business people that had breakdowns. Some customers would love to drive a business broke and then buy it real cheap.

Many customers told me that there was something wrong with the newspapers and TV. (Did they mean "mixed messages?") One customer told me that you only have to attract 30 or 40 people to get media attention "Some people will do anything to get on television!" **I'm convinced that sections of the media and Government made a lot of money out of our personal lives and problems.** The media is a completely ruthless and cut-throat, mixed message, hangman stir.

Several people told me "I'm leaving the area before this all blows up in their faces"

Someone once told me that buying groceries is a "grudge buy" Hunger forces people to go to a shop and forces them to spend the money. A customer once told me "the world would be a different place if we didn't have to eat"

Also people who get abused with money and have emotional problems are usually reckless spenders.

One customer told us "if you make people pay, you will lose business faster than if you cheat them" Oh what problems you have if you don't get paid on time - let alone in good faith! Oh what problems you have if you can't pay what you owe!

> In 1971, the average family grocery bill was probably about $40 a week. In 2018, it's probably around $300 a week. We should have had a "Budget Advice Service" that tried to cut our customers' household, business or farming costs. **It would have been the same as free groceries – the same as giving them the money to shop with us. It took me 30 years to think of this.** Any business can start a "Budget Advice Service" – including a Football Club. How smart was it for an AFL team to appoint a high profile, media financial advisor as its CEO?

Any-way, when- ever I shop, I always re-live the experiences – both good and bad - so I decided to write this.

MISCELLANEOUS BUSINESS STORIES

Over a 57 year, work-life, I was sometimes told the three main components of a happy and healthy business, workplace and budget.

- Put the Lord first (the 1st Commandment) Do things His way. Glorify His name and work for Him. He is your main employer. Many people who don't believe still have a very strong focus on serving others in their local community.
(The 2nd Commandment) (Love Thy Neighbour)
- Produce a diligent work effort that is in Good Faith. Have honest financial transactions that are also in Good Faith
- The first thing to do with any increase is to make your offerings to the Lord or (if you don't believe) offerings to others in your community

The above sows a good seed. "What you sow is what you reap" (Gal 6: 7-9)

Miscellaneous Business Stories

<u>Story No.1.</u> In 1968, as a 15-year-old, my first school holiday job was in a deli across the road from the Adelaide Children's Hospital. The place attracted some real undesirables. The owner was very street savvy and spent a lot of time talking about sex (before talking promiscuity became fashionable) She sometimes set me up for stealing, but my parents instilled in me a sense of honesty and I was clean.

<u>Story No.2.</u> For over nine years, my parents owned two deli's and a small country town general store. We thought all we need to do is run an honest business that sold good quality good s as cheaply as we could. How wrong we were! It was hundreds of 12 to 16-hour days. A wasted work effort because the big profits aren't there in groceries. Your business is also your home and it was like having several hundred strangers walk in to your lounge room every day (24/7) They were still the days before Australia had a major drug and alcohol problem. Then there was all the verbal abuse and physically violent threats

---

I learned the 80/20 rule. Only 5% of any given demographic cause all the problems. Another 15% get caught up in the upsets and arguments (which blow up out of all proportion). The remaining 80% just mind their own business or don't care. I think it is also a good way of looking at the rash, useless generalization that is called "racism"

Some of our business highlights were

- The nasty, bizarre and degrading personal attacks and invasion of privacy. The degrading sexism and how some (not all) customers laughed in your face.

(like demon possessed hyenas suffering from Mad Cow's Disease) The threats of physical violence.

- The petty theft. WE had to stop some customers from helping themselves to packets of cigarettes, putting the money in the till themselves, and giving themselves their own change

- Upsets about customers insisting on their absolute legal right to unlimited and indefinite credit. One customer told me "if you make people pay (their accounts) you will lose business faster than if you cheat them!"

- Also, the media and advertising lackeys were no good. You only need to attract 30 or 40 people to get media attention. Many customers told me that some of the stories in the papers and television were no good. Does the media fuel a fire with "hangman" mixed messages? Does it perpetuate a stir? Is there such a thing as "hangman mixed message character assassination?" "Some people will do anything to get on television"

We should have had a budget advice service. (BAS) If we could have trimmed our customers' household, business, or farming budget, it would have been the same as free groceries. The same as giving them the money to shop with us! Any business can have a Budget Advice Service. (including a football club) Monthly cost cutting social evenings would also benefit a small community. Why did it take me over 30 years of living in the past to think of this???? A teacher at High School called us Numb Skulls!

Story No.3. My parents sold their General Store in Aug of 1982 and I had a working holiday in Queensland. (hoping to become a better guitar player) I had seen all the tourism ads with the beautiful girls on the beautiful beaches and got this stupid idea in my head that only happy people lived there.

An elderly female Gold Coast real estate agent warned me "you be very careful here. This place has got a real reputation for attracting the worst people in Australia" Other people also warned me to be careful. You'd think that I would have gotten to know them. Why couldn't I remember what they said 10 minutes later? Why does it come crashing down on me years later?

Story No.4. I got a job selling printing and the owners and staff were really good to me. None-the-less, they wouldn't have thought twice about pulling a dodgy shonk. They spent a long time teaching me how to sell but I was told "every-one rips everyone else off - especially here on the Gold Coast" "if a guitar player gets asked to go to the States, every time he plays a wrong chord, it gets ripped off his wages"

I really enjoyed the job but left when their finances didn't look right. Maybe they were laundering money. Also, I couldn't tell if I was or wasn't involved in the then "Bottom of the Harbor" tax scam

Story No.5. I then worked in a chicken shop and the two owner brothers and workmates were good to me - except for the occasional vitriolic personal attack. They were very astute business men and they knew how much would be in their till based on percentages and the number of chickens they sold every day. It was how they could tell if any of the staff were stealing. Later, their accountant understated the amount of tax I paid by two amounts of $40 ($400 in 2021 values.) So, when they fired me without reason, I lodged a complaint. Never again! The upset wasn't worth it. They did other good things for me and they didn't deserve it. I ended up being ashamed of what happened.

Story No.6 After that I worked as a kitchen hand/cleaner in Bonaparte's Hotel in Brisbane. It was a great job (despite some of the fights that broke out) The hotel was always packed with noisy, boisterous uni. students. It was a mixed message head-stuff when the media promoted the song "Bonaparte's Retreat" (by Glen Campbell) From other comments that were made to me I should have guessed that I was getting media attention. Who knows why.

It was around March of 1983 - around the time Bob Hawke was first elected. I got told that the Aust. dollar fell five cents (before it was floated) because of something that happened in Queensland at that time. Who knows what? When I got fired from the chicken shop, I just dismissed the boss as a "bum who didn't recognize talent." Later my head was stuffed and I went paranoid when Bob Hawke wore his black & white newspaper headline jacket and cracked his America's Cup "bum boss" joke. I always had trouble telling fact from fiction.

Despite some bizarre and degrading incidents, I enjoyed my time in Queensland (trying to be a better guitar player). However, I must have been a bit naive and happy-go-lucky. I was only on the DOLE for a few weeks and once got a letter from Social Security asking me to explain myself. It looked like someone was fraudulently claiming benefits using my name. Also, everything messes up if I myself and others, get impersonated in phone calls. A lot of nasty stuff must have happened behind my back and 38 years later, I still have nightmares about ever finding out.

Story No.7. In August of 1983, I got offered a very low paying job in Canberra – with the Govt Car Fleet (COMCAR, Transport & Storage Division and the Dept of Administrative Services). I didn't know that I accidentally walked straight into a political hornet's nest. A lot of my workmates told me that there is something wrong with this place and nobody knows what it is. I copped that comment in just about every place I ever worked or lived. I must have been a bit naive and happy-go-lucky to live in Canberra & never read a news-paper or watch TV. One workmate bluntly told me "it costs $32 an hour to run a Govt Car and $14 an hour to hire a taxi (1985 values) She then just walked off and left me sitting there by myself. I later suspected that the figures were reported in the media. If you make rash, useless, generalizations it implies that over half of the Public Service budget was either wasted or defrauded.

T&S Div. was one bizarre and degrading incident after another. Everything came crashing down on me on the night of my birthday in 1985. I didn't know where I was and in all the confusion registered two business names (to work as a session musician) (a Home-Based Micro Business) I got trashed in the media even before I got the registration certificates. I won't play music for an upset and when I canceled, I got told that I "f***ed them all up" 36 years later, I still don't know what happened.

There were many other things wrong, I had a nasty bullying problem and was very ill. I lost my Public Service job and got kicked out of Canberra. Some of my workmates didn't like what was done to me, but others couldn't contain themselves laughing – like demon possessed hyenas suffering from Mad Cow's Disease. After a transfer back to Adelaide, I spent another 7 years in the Public Service and then in 1994, either left or got kicked out again.

The last I heard of the Dept of Admin Services was that some (not all) of the staff were flying themselves all over the country – claiming that they were at the ground-breaking for-front of the ground-breaking New Age creative business thinking. The Canberra power brokers then weeded out so much dead wood that the Dept was weeded out of all existence. Even after applying the 80/20 Rule it was a dishonest, fraudulent, degrading, workplace.

I later got told if you leave the Public Service or trash an ex-employer you'll never work again. 27 years later, in 2021, I never had a full- time income again. I managed on casual work and a partial Disability Pension. Australia must be a rich country to support such a life style.

Story No.8. In 1985, the government created the New Enterprise Incentive Scheme. (NEIS.) Since then, many people have started a Home-Based Micro Business from their garage or a spare room. All you need is a good idea and a business plan. It's not hard to set something up that negative gears (offsets or pays) $20,000 p.a. of expenses. That's a lot of money if you're on the pension.

Story No.9. It's now 2021, & I have played and taught guitar part time, after hours, for 58 years. Musicians and others have worked from home for centuries. (the first Home Based Micro Business????) I have many stories about the music business (or do I mean musical fraud?)

Many teenagers have limited musical abilities and no media or business skills. They are approached by dubious producers who try and find out if they have wealthy parents or an inheritance from their grandfather.

One talent show contestant was told "you didn't win, but we liked what we saw and would like to develop your talent" He was promised the world, got promoted, & **"bought"** a recording contract, He sold 300,000 units @$30 and turned over nine million dollars. His contract however, was so stitched up that he didn't get paid a cent

"Contract rip off" stories like that, circulated for years before they made the headlines (springing the game) So, now-a-days nobody wants a record deal.

It's the same with the publishing game. The contracts are that complicated, if the author makes one little mistake, he has broken the agreement and doesn't get paid at all.

Story No.10 I think Australia put a curse on itself when Valentine's Day (14/2/66) was chosen as the Decimal Currency Change-over Date. "The love of money is at the root of all evil" (1 Tim 6:10) Are we supposed to love each other with money and laugh our financial problems off as a joke? The first day of the new financial year would have been a more logical choice. By freak coincidence, the advertising jingle (sung to Click Go the Shears) was the 1st or 2nd song my brother and I played in public (as youngsters in 1965)

Story No.11 Two of the world's biggest problems are greed and coveting. If you think an accountant has a boring job, try sorting out a fraud problem. The perpetrators have to do a lot else wrong to cover their tracks and the paper trail. The associated confusion, degrading sexism, often violent abuse and racism are something to behold.

A HOME-BASED MICRO-BUSINESS.

Did I Set a Precedent?
(Is this believable?)

How did this Blow Up out
of All Proportion?

How did this Blow Up out of All Proportion?

A Home-Based Micro-business.
<u>Did I Set a Precedent?</u> (Is this believable?)

As a teenager in the 60's, I always wanted a relatively easy life as a school teacher, researcher or mathematician. Then after many bizarre and degrading incidents, my science career at Adelaide University messed up. I didn't realize that it messed up big time. Mixed message newspaper articles like the "psychologist broken nose" and "pet rock" stories should have told me so Also the Dark Glasses story. Am I going nuts here or what?

Was all my personal life a mixed message, hangman, advertising and media stir? Did my problems first start in kindergarten - just after I got molested by a teenage girl? (c1958)

After a poor attempt at addressing my problems, I locked myself away in my room with a blind obsession of becoming a better guitar player. What a mistake! Never again! - but that's another story

From 1983 to 1994, I was a Commonwealth Public Servant - both in Canberra and here in Adelaide. I also taught guitar part- time, after hours. Again, after many bizarre and degrading incidents, I didn't know where I was. In my confusion, I registered the business names of "Opal Music" and "Dawn Music" (IN Canberra in 1985)

I figured that if I minded my own business and kept to myself with a Home-based Micro-business, then my enemies would look like trash.

I got trashed on the air and by strangers in the street - even before I got the Business Registration Certificates. You should have heard the uncontrollable, hysterical laughter – like demon possessed hyenas suffering from Mad Cow's Disease. Years later, I heard one television host say "we're still laughing at that joke we played on that guy – fair go tho' – he was on the verge of a breakdown." The main reason people laugh at others is so they can forgot how stupid they look themselves. I'm fairly certain that several media stars played more than one joke on me and they all back fired.

I assume it was genuine when, by freak chance, (on a radio sound grab) I heard Peter Garrett (Midnight Oil) say "the guy who did Opal Music thinks it's all forgotten but at the age of 40, Bruce Springstein still does four hour concerts" I didn't even know what that meant. Did the media play "hangman" with me? I didn't think of ringing the radio station and asking "is the media playing Cat & Mouse with me?" Several years later I read that at the time Midnight Oil got onto the Letterman Show in New York and gave a "memorable performance"

My late father told me that what I did was so unusual that nobody knew what to do. "Be careful you don't lose everything you have"

People promote Equal Opportunity. How many leeches suck the blood out of a stone? It cost me a lot of money and I don't play music for a stir – so I cancelled both names. I got told that I "f***ed them all up" with no explanation of what that meant.

It was 1986. I lost my Public Service job, got kicked out of Canberra and lost a lot of money.

How can this blow up out of all proportion? Here is some of what happened afterwards

- Was there a bizarre "earplug" incident on TV? Did I see that right?
- The Govt set up the NEIS Scheme (New Enterprise Incentive Scheme)
- Musical bands had to register their names as business names.
- The Dept. of Social Security (later Centrelink) called its computer system "OPAL" (On-line Policy & Legislation) I got several comments of "those f***heads ruined everything"
- Now and then there is an article in the paper about how, if someone has a problem, "then some lazy, overpaid, Public Service rock ape turns it into a policy
- The Tax Dept. had to amend its legislation and forms to allow for people who had a Home- based Micro-Business. (over a 30 year period) E.g. They had to stop people claiming a business loss against other income. E.g. one year over 600,000 people listed their occupation as "musician." The ATO had to change its "occupation" question to "what was the major source of your income?"
- Govt. departments were broken up into business units that had to show a profit – as was my own employer Dept. (Comcar & Admin Services) Some of the staff flew themselves all over the country – claiming that they were at the ground-breaking fore-front of the New Age Creative Corporate Business Thinking.
- Many private corporations were also broken up into business units.
- Accounting was changed from cost centres to profit centres.
- There was a business in England named "Opal Music" There is also an "Opal Music Studio" in the States

- It was a mixed message head stuff when A Current Affair did a story about "Opal Re-cycled Medicines"
- I have a diverse work history with a lot of basic skills in a lot of different areas. The Public Service made a big deal of "multi-skilling"
- At the same time that I had these problems the policy makers created their EO, OH&S, Workplace Relations, Enterprise Bargaining, and Industrial Democracy Policies.
- I suspect that I got into a racism argument which I didn't want to know about.
- There was a lot of suspicion about who gets awards – especially design awards. Many awards were given to independent musicians, independent filmmakers and other independents. Did I set a precedent for this?
- There was a media plethora of "don't give up your day job" and "conflict of interest" stories
- There was a suspicious article in the paper which suggested that Alan Bond paid less tax on his entire fortune than I did on my part-time music teaching job
- Did my government employer get a specific mention on an American Music Award show? Was the comment "there's more going on there than there ever was in Dallas" (the 1980's TV Show) Did I see that right?
- My Public Service employer organised a "How to Handle the Media" Conference and flew delegates into Canberra from all over Australia. I would have liked to attend but, instead, they sent me on a course to teach me how to answer a phone. (In those days call centres didn't exist)
- Around 1994, there was an upset in Adelaide about the "Aboriginal Secret Women's Business" The Advertiser Newspaper rang my ex-supervisor about the matter. After querying whether she gave her correct name, she got splashed on the front page

because of the way she answered the phone and the way she spoke to the press. The reporter ended his story by writing "Oh what secrets we keep!"

- I often meet people who tell me that their employer pays many thousands of dollars to external consultants to conduct in-house training courses. Some of the staff just get up and go to the toilet.

- I met a disability worker who showed me one of her government manuals. I recognized some of the content as the work I had done with my students. The disability worker just sneered at the manual and told me that she had to go to the toilet. I also became suspicious of the background production and politics of Adelaide produced disability films like "Shine" and "The King's Speech"

Around 1988, we had a week end get-away holiday at the Opal Fields in Andamooka. When we walked into the hotel it was deathly quiet and some one asked me if I was "doing business" Then a five year old girl came up to me and interfered with herself – right in the middle of the room" **Never Again!** It must have been strange Education Dept background thinking when a friend and her husband were appointed as principals of a neighbouring town school.

I don't know what else happened. I dread ever finding out

Who writes what, where the ideas come from, and who gets paid cause some massive, bitter and nasty arguments – especially if it involves drugs and alcohol, an invasion of privacy or a personal attack.

Was all my personal life a mixed message, hangman, advertising and media stir? Did my problems first start in kindergarten - just after I got molested by a teenage girl? (c1958)

<u>EVERYTHING CAME CRASHING DOWN on ME</u>

Did I get shown some dodgy fraudulent videos? "Nobody would remember that" Did I see that right?

- Did I see "too far to go" and "stars have to be helped" stories on TV? Did I see that right"
- I fell ill
- I got laughed at and trashed in the media. You should have heard the uncontrollable hysterical laughter – like demon possessed hyenas suffering from Mad Cow's Disease! It stank like dingo shit
- My family and friends also got laughed at and trashed
- Did I myself and other people get impersonated?
- I suspected that my phone was tapped and that I was the victim of a listening device.
- I copped all sorts of bizarre and degrading remarks – including that I was a paedophile and was too lazy to work. It didn't look right when I got set up alone with some women and children.
- I got psyched out by a lot of idiot, contrived, body language.
- People told me "you're gonna' get yours" "talk about a country shooting itself in the foot because it forgets about the money" useless generalisations like "all Australians are bastards" "they're all in on it" "my mother wants me to be a rock star and she bashes me" "it sucks"
- I never really had an income again after I either left or got kicked out of the Public Service in 1994

It seems to me, that, if there is a problem some managers produce a useless Public Relations stir.
(a sort of Trial by Media)

They claim they repeatedly tried to "reach out" to the other party but got no response.

Sometimes a manager publishes a photo of himself standing in the middle of a bridge across a river.

When I've had my name dropped on air, nobody has ever bothered to "reach out" to me at all.

When I had all the problems in my Public Service job, the Area Manager came to the depot to talk to me and nobody told me he was there.

A lot of wealthy people advertised their art form in the 1985 Aboriginal Reconciliation Walk across the Sydney Harbour Bridge. Nobody bothered to address the basic Aboriginal financial problems.

You'd think that if I had these problems then I would be offered a well-paid job. All I get is Intellectual Property problems. All the good jobs go to other people and I get left sitting there by myself – wondering what happened?

Now and then there is an article in the paper about how "If some-one has a problem, then some lazy over-paid Public Service rock ape turns it into a policy" I once told a female Public Service workmate that she was better at her job than I was at mine. Later she accused me of carrying on like I was the only one who did any work around the place. I knew plenty of competent Public Servants who were better at their jobs than I was at mine. Everyone's different!!

Again, am I entitled to a well-paid job in the government or media? Am I entitled to an "Act of Grace" compensation payment from both of them?

P.S. I've had a Home Based Micro Business since 1984 and mostly turn over between 5 and 20 thousand dollars a year (2019 values) It's a lot of money if you're on the pension

BIZARRE AND DEGRADING COMMENTS

Over the years, I copped many bizarre and degrading comments, and suffered many incidents.

I mostly blanked out and couldn't remember them for decades. Then years later, they come crashing down on me.

I make a bad mistake of living in the past. I have a ship wreck of a memory, that only surfaces at low tide. I have bad comprehension skills and no diplomatic gift of the gab. I sometimes live in a shell (like a crab of my Zodiac Sign) and everything just bounces off. I can't hear anything and can't see past the end of my nose. I swim in a very small pool.

I had a lot of trouble asserting and defending myself.

I fall ill one or two days a week, then I sort of recover and manage my affairs O.K.

I always try and remember the 80/20 Rule. Only 5% of any given demographic cause all the problems. Another 15% get caught up in the upsets and arguments which blow up out of all proportion. The remaining 80% just mind their own business and don't care. It's not a bad way of looking at the fraud that is racism.

I think in the 50's & 60's people had a different way of speaking to each other. There was an emphasis on good manners and being polite. If you said "bloody" you were scorned and I don't think the "F" & "C" words existed.

The media had a different way of addressing an audience. Individuals weren't singled out and addressed directly. People were addressed as "listeners, viewers, or members of the audience" Bob and Dolly Dyer in their BP Pick-a-Box Show would say "customers"

In the late 60's, one Adelaide television host turned his studio monitor around to show the audience that it only showed the inside of his studio. He couldn't see people in their homes.

Around 2010, a viewer wrote into the Channel 10 News. "I don't like the way the news readers are looking at me. Tell them to stop it"

The early television films had a disclaimer at the end which more or less said "The characters and events depicted in this film are entirely fictitious. Any resemblance to a person living or dead, is purely coincidence"

- I was always badly bullied at school – as was my younger brother. Maybe I brought it on myself, because, on the surface, I was an arrogant, cheeky, smart aleck. I don't think other German children copped it any where near as bad as I did
I associated with one of the school bullies for 37 years before I realized what he was like. What he did is unfit to write about.
At the end of the day, every bully suffers for what he does. You can't sink the boot into them when they're on the ground. "What you sow, is what you reap) (Gal 6: 7-9)

- Everything messes up if I myself, and others get impersonated in phone calls.

- I had many years of associating with the SA Education Dept. and had no idea that the Dept. attracted so many perverted, sexual deviates.
  I had a medical in my first week at Teacher's College and the Doctor was unethical.
  In 1971, I had an initial week's teaching experience at Norwood Primary School. As an inexperienced 17-year-old, I was left alone on Yard Duty, while the other staff had a social lunch. I didn't see it, when one of the parents came into the yard and hassled a pupil.
  A student told me that that one of the 12-year old girls cries herself to sleep over me every night. I felt quite ill and had to forget about that real quick.
  For whatever reason, Norwood Primary School was closed and not re-opened for at least 30 years.
  Later, one of my peers asked me "what do you do if a 7-year old girl tells you she loves you?"
  I didn't take the question seriously and just groaned and replied "here's my card kid. Give us a ring in twenty years" Several years later, the joke got repeated to me by a stranger. It didn't click that I had those sorts of problems.

- There were many bizarre and degrading incidents in our deli's (c1971- 1982) We had to ask a lady not to sit her dog on our flat top milk & ice-cream fridge. She responded with a vitriolic Nazi salute, screamed out Zeig Heil" and stormed out. I wish I would have asked her "do you wear swastika em-broided underwear?"

- Over the years, I heard many bizarre stories about what happens in a public toilet – especially in the Education Dept. I never wanted to know about them – let alone be part of them

- Once I was walking past a deserted library and a group of students lined me up. They bluntly told me that I got called a "wanker" at Government House, and then, marched off in single file, leaving me standing there. I just blanked out and couldn't remember the incident for years.

  Then 12 years later, in 1985, did I get shown a fraudulent video? Was I shown an old, black & white, student film? Did it show me being called a wanker in a Government House dinner party scene? Was the tag at the end "no-body would remember that?

- Once a stranger uni. student invited me to a party. I told her I couldn't go because I had to start work at 4.00 am Sunday morning. The Monday after the party, she came up to me, full of vitriol, and threatened to break my nose. I was stunned and blurted out the first stupid thing that came to my head. "People with broken noses make better lovers!" A couple of weeks later, there was a one paragraph article in the paper saying "a psychologist said people with broken noses make better lovers" After that there were many one paragraph articles in the paper which started with "a psychologist said" or a "psychiatrist said" They stuffed my head and it didn't click that they came from me

- I was once walking through a deserted campus and a stranger asked me "what do you think of ASIO agents using concealed cameras to photograph anti-war protestors"? I replied "it's a bugs bunny cartoon, with the spy wearing dark glasses, hiding behind a newspaper. They wouldn't like it if they had their own photos taken" A couple of weeks later, the paper published the photos of about a dozen ASIO agents on the front page – some wearing their dark glasses.

Over many years many people tried to psyche me out with their dark glasses.

- At Uni, in 1973, I had a lot of problems with a fellow student – a teenage girl who screamed at me for a period of nine months. The noise was unbearable – even from a hundred meters away. I was completely destroyed by the way I got laughed at. A classic example of what's wrong with the Equal Opportunity Act.
Years later, I had a different understanding of why a man loses his self-control, and, hits a woman. Delegating, to another female, the job of a punch in the face, isn't right either.
What her script writer brother wrote in the "Chicken Man" radio series is unknown to me. I often got called a "chicken" as did other people that I knew.
About a year later, I saw the same thing done to the Skyhooks Rock Band.
Years later, the same thing was done to Kerry Packer and Senator Gareth Evans. I suspect that later, the girl suffered for all that screaming she did.

- Once in 1976, I went to the beach. My Education Dept. supervisor was also there, and his two bouncer mates over powered me, removed my bathers and left me there naked in the crowd. I blanked out, froze, and couldn't remember the incident 10 minutes later. I had no chance against two bouncers and must have been in a state of shock.
I didn't realize that I had Legal Rights and that it was a straight-out case of "Indecent Assault" Years later, I remembered, that at work, the following Monday, the supervisor told me that his girlfriend was extremely upset. I think he was extremely worried and ashamed and tried to make amends. I just couldn't remember,

but what happened behind the scenes must have been very nasty.

- **One doctor told me that my biggest talent was helping people with depression. Another doctor told me that people were interested in my ability with words.** I was too run down and exhausted to ask what they meant. Nor could I remember 10 minutes later. The implication was that I had Intellectual Property and plagiarism problems.

- In March of 1977, my parents bought a small country town General Store. The business was a complete mess. Many customers insisted on their God Given right to unlimited, indefinite credit, and the place was just about to go broke because of the state of its accounts.
In the first week, one of the local females threw a couple of empty cartons at my feet, sneered "there's a couple of boxes for you" and stormed out. I was completely destroyed.
Degrading sexist language wasn't around in those days. It was usually known as the "double entendre" that was spoken by homosexuals.
Anyway, the woman gave me a complete working over for 18 months. Everything was mixed messages, the idiot contrived body language, and the stony facial expressions. Then she would just walk off and leave me standing there – spluttering. A pig of a way to behave in someone's business and home.
Another classic example of what's wrong with the Equal Opportunity Act.

- Once a customer laughed at me badly – three mornings in a row. I lost my temper and sprayed him with "F" & "C" words. I kept screaming "this man is an a**e-h*le and the paint just about blistered off the walls. He was a lot tougher and stronger than I was but he didn't retaliate because I caught him by surprise. Years later, I couldn't believe it when the same scene was repeated in a movie – except the abuse was directed at the shop-keeper.

- I was the butt of jokes to a lot of people. (not all) One woman laughed at everything I said and did for five and a half years. What is so funny about putting a jar of cream or bottle of sauce on a counter? Why snigger at that? I mostly just blanked out and once, lost control of my bowels – just because of the way she laughed in my face. I couldn't remember the incident ten minutes later.

 The only consolation I have is that I've heard of that happening to other people.

 Over the years, I heard stories about the disproportionate number of small business owners who had breakdowns because of what their customers and other business men did to them.

 Another classic example of what's wrong with the Equal Opportunity Act!

 You have to forgive and leave people alone for mistakes they made years ago, but at the time I should have also told her "your teenage daughter has a very stupid way of buying an ice-cream.

Her husband sometimes stirred me up - e.g. calling me the "petrol jerk" So I asked him a few hard questions and he was visibly agitated. I only told one person that story and a couple of weeks later a local reporter published a story on the front page of the local paper. He had interviewed another local business man and wrote that the business man was "visibly agitated at the hard questions" It didn't click at the time, that my personal life was being spread all over the place.

- The husband/father was generally a decent guy who tried to meet us on middle ground – despite not liking what we did. We thought it was funny when once, after a bit of mutual friction he blurted out, "why don't you brown shirts be nice to your customers?" The family never really did anything wrong but years later I was spewing when I saw her (or a look-a-like) in a Christian, dinner table, television ad. A couple of years after we sold, he told my brother "you apologize to Harry for what was done to him! Make sure you tell him that – the next time you see him!"

- I had one customer walk in and say "you t**d! I'll have a packet of Wingfield (cigarettes) and hurry up about it". Anyone else would have just slammed his head through their front door, but he did it three times before I defended myself. I don't think I look too good if I play hangman. i.e. give 40 years of rope, then tighten the noose when I write my memoirs.

- Every year, the Volkswagen Club Car Rally used us as a Check Point and we had to run around everywhere – trying to get everyone served. Once a customer kept laughing at me "there's mother hen Harry." So, I touch his chin with me fist and his mouth straightened out. I touched a little harder and it turned upside down. I touched harder again, and he started to sweat and then walked off. Later another customer told me "if I had to work like that and got laughed at, I would have done exactly the same thing!"

- Around the year 2000, the town was featured in a front-page story in the Sunday Mail. A local and his wife, while holidaying in ASIA, were kidnapped by rebels. The captives told some stories of where the came from. The rebels laughed that hard, gave them

$10, and sent them home in a taxi. Unbelievable! How I wish I had kept the article!

- 26 years after we sold, I was sitting at a bus stop and two strangers walked by. They laughed good naturedly, and commented "they used to own a small country town General Store. They closed all their customers' accounts and all the locals couldn't wait to get rid of the bastards. Then when they sold it, absolutely everything f***ed up, and all the locals wanted them back there. That's what's going on!"

- When I lived on the Gold Coast, my elderly land agent warned me "you be very careful here! This place has got a real reputation for attracting the worst people in Australia" Other people also warned me to be careful, but I couldn't remember what they said ten minutes later. You'd think I would have gotten to know them.

- When I first moved to Canberra, I was in a bar, and a stranger came up to me. "I don't know what you've done, but I'd get out of here, real quick. Those guys over there want to beat the hell out of you"

- A female co-worker put a sex shop purchased wax penis on my birthday cake. A couple of weeks later, some Sydney demonstrators organised a protest featuring a gigantic penis on a gigantic birthday cake. It didn't click that my problems had blown out of all proportion. Several years later, the female co-worker was filmed in a 60 Minutes Story, making an over the counter purchase in a sex shop. Several years after that we both accidentally went to the same pub in the Riverland. You should have heard the uncontrollable hysterical laugher as she kept repeating "He's here! He's here!" Like a demon possessed hyena, suffering from Mad Cow's Disease!

- The comments I got about the 1985 BHP "Big Australian" ad was "The Big Hun."
  The comments I got about the BHP "Quiet Achiever" ads were "The Quiet Deceiver."
  The were produced by Bell Resources and I got other funny isolated comments about what they did.

Everything came crashing down on me, in Canberra, on the night of my birthday. (Friday, 13/7/85).

The Live band Aid Concert was broad-cast the same evening.

I couldn't find the jumper that I was given as an early birthday present and George Negus was wearing an identical one.

Both he and Molly Meldrum made personal comments about me – e.g. "he's just put an ad in the paper" and "we got out of that one"

The show was full of the idiot, contrived body language, and was extended for an hour, because "the Russians joined in"

At the end, there were two different sound coming out of my television set – one of the broad-cast and the other my guitar playing (or similar)

Several months later, I was shown a video extract which showed a group of farmers weeping because they had shot the wrong guy. I was told "it came through at three o'clock in the morning"

- **I almost collapsed twice. A doctor told me "Often when people have a shock like that, they just drop dead on the spot"**

- Did I see a "too far to go" and "stars have to be helped" story?

- I got comments of "You're gonna get yours" and "you're gonna get what you deserve" When I asked what that meant, they just walked off and left me standing there.

- I got comments of "talk about a country shooting itself in the foot, because it forgets about the money"

- There must have been something wrong with the way I got set up alone with some women and children. Strangers in the street called me a "paedophile" on several occasions. There was a particularly nasty situation when an hysterical women kept repeatedly screaming at me "go on dirt! Find yourself a five-year old"

- It must have been around 1997, when I applied for a Volunteer Job. My interview was at 5.00 pm and I was unable to explain why the entire City of Adelaide was deserted (right in the middle of Rush Hour) All I saw was two people, who laughed at me, as they entered a building.

- I got comments, in German, of "Das is Der" and "Das Australischen Schieze"

- I once took my guitar to a party, a lady had one look at me, and got instantly upset. As soon as people get upset or excited, they make useless, rash, generalizations" She exclaimed "All Australians are bastards"

- I heard a couple of Adelaide television personalities comment "I didn't write everything I wanted in my autobiography, because I didn't want to trash a lot of people. All he wanted was to be left alone."

In 1985, my problems were that bad that I almost collapsed twice. One doctor told me "often if a person has an experience or shock like that, they just drop dead on the spot!"

In 1985 I lost my Public Service job and got kicked out of Canberra Enthusiastically encouraged to seek greener pastures elsewhere! Years later, two comments struck home.

1. A weather reporter said "All politicians should be turned into homeless buskers and be made to sing for their supper"
2. An Australian international soccer player said he was called into his manager's office. The manager told him "I owe you $50,000 but I'm not going to pay you. Instead, I'll give you a clean sheet and you can go anywhere in the world you want.

After I got a transfer back to Adelaide, I was laughed at badly by a couple of female co-workers.

They were disgusting comments and disgusting laughter by females promoting EO.

Later, I called it "The 1987 Merry Christmas Laugh"

I lost my temper badly and sprayed the office with a full-on barrage of F & C words. The paint just about blistered off the walls. The receptionist asked me to settle down and the manager sent me home and told me to get a medical certificate. When I went back to work a couple of weeks later, I didn't know where I was. One of the female managers (AMT) came up to me and said "if you ever feel like you're going to lose your temper like that again, come and see me first so that it doesn't happen again." How decent was she? I was a numb skull who didn't appreciate what she said and did.

I don't really bear any bitterness to most of the Public Servants I worked with. Most (not all) are only doing their jobs. The other staff told me "this is a hornet's nest of a fraudulent, toxic, workplace"

One of the managers must have done himself considerable damage when he told the office that I should be kicked in the groin for leaving the lid to the photocopier up. I complained to another supervisor, but she was his good mate and just told me "the dust gets on the glass" Then I couldn't remember the incident 10 minutes later. I didn't realize that it was serious and legitimate complaint

One 18-year old (Pat) just sat quietly at his desk and worked steadily away all day. If he had a cup of coffee, he drank it while he was working. Occasionally he would tell me something, and I thought he was better at his job than I was.

One of the managers (Tony) always said hello to me decently and it didn't occur to me to get to know him.

I went to head Office several times and complained but was mostly degraded.

I complained about the wax penis on the birthday cake, and the female EO Officer just sneered at me and asked me "just exactly what sort of a job would you like?"

A union rep spent 30 seconds listening to my complaint, bluntly told me that I was the next Governor General of Australia, and shut the door in my face.

One senior staffer in head office told me "if you want us to handle this for you, just let us know"

The Area Manager came to my depot to talk to me and nobody told me he was there.

One manager, who was still quite young, called me into his office and asked me "are you unhappy because we've slotted you into the debtor's job?" I replied "no I could use a change" and he said "that's the easiest problem I ever had to solve"

THE JOY OF ESCAPISM

Escape from a Bad Habit

SMOKING – How I got Hooked

In 1968, As a 15-year-old teenager, the first tune that I could play by ear on my guitar, was "The Marlboro Man." About a year later, another cigarette ad appeared featuring my Christian name of Harald (Harold????)
A very cunning stunt!
We ridiculed the ad by imitation and role play and then lit up with a Marlboro. I started for a joke and the taste was that bad, that I never thought that I would get hooked. Satan is very good at back-firing a joke (especially with drugs and alcohol) 50 years later I still have chronic problems.

Sometimes I crack, and consider taking legal action to recover medical costs & other damages. Cigarette companies however, will deny it. They have more money to pay more powerful lawyers. I'll never win!

In 1971, when we owned our first deli, I told my father that we didn't look too good selling cigarettes to children in school uniform. We all agreed and stopped the practice. Then, two weeks later, my head was stuffed when legislation was rushed through SA Parliament, banning the sale of cigarettes to minors.

My head was again stuffed - 20 years later - (c1991) Adelaide's Today Tonight Show set up and sprung, the then owner of the same Deli, for selling cigarettes to minors. Later I was told me that there was a dis-proportionate number of media stories coming from the same area.

> I also have many other mixed message, hangman, marketing and media problems.
>
> **Does the media fuel a fire and perpetuate a stir with hangman, mixed message, character assassination? (Double-think. Double-speak. Portmanteau????)**
> **- or do the politicians and other people do that themselves?**
>
> **At the time of the Russian Revolution, Lenin & Marx formulated a 10 Point Plan to destabilize the West. I could never find a copy and read what's in it. I know however, that one of the destabilizing components is drugs & alcohol.**
>
> **Was all my life a mixed message, hangman media and advertising stir? Did my problems first start in kindergarten (c1958) – just after I was molested by a teenage girl?**

It is almost impossible to **stop a bad habit - (e.g.** smoking, alcohol, eating disorders etc.) by the **Willpower Method.**
- by fighting the cravings. (fight or flight)

Here is an easier way! (based on escapism) (using the example of smoking)
Escapism to a happy place is a basic component of the human psyche

> Refer Allen Carr's Books & Videos "The Easy Way to Stop Smoking"
> It's a completely different approach and different way of thinking. He has a 95% Success Rate.

<u>Keep Repeating to Yourself (loudly)</u> (even while continuing to smoke, drink, or the bad habit)

- I will not concede and convince myself that I am a smoker. I will convince myself that I am a non-smoker. (by positive auto-suggestion and positive affirmation)
- (Yippee!) and/or (Hallelujah & Praise the Lord!) I am a happy, healthy, non-smoker who has escaped
- There are no cravings or withdrawal symptoms. I only think there are. It is the Great Nicotine Con. I will not convince myself that there are cravings and withdrawal symptoms. It is the Great Nicotine Con.
- I have escaped the misery, sickness and bondage of the Great Nicotine Con
- When I light that first cigarette I am putting a little monster in my body. It is always hungry and keeps screaming out "Feed me! Feed me! Feed me with more cigarettes and nicotine." I need to starve him to death. I need to starve him out of my body" (Refer Allen Carr)
- There is no such thing as "just one more cigarette. Just one more cigarette is a lifetime of misery, sickness & bondage
- I do not understand that, if I light up just one more cigarette, it will cost me tens of thousands of dollars – maybe hundreds of thousands!
- I can't keep myself clean. If I have just one more disgusting, filthy, cigarette, it is a lifetime of disgusting filth. I am missing out on happy, healthy, cleanliness
- Lighting up to have a break, is the wrong form of escapism! If I light up, I will be in a sick, miserable place. I will not escape to a happy, healthy place.
- Do I enjoy the ceremony of lighting up? No! I do not!
- Can I go without? Of course, I can!
- Do I need this cigarette? Of course not! Smoking is not a reward but a dirty filthy habit.

- Do I enjoy smoking? No! I do not! When I smoke, I will not drink. I will not think happy thoughts.
- I have an unhappy smoking place where I keep my filthy cigarettes.
- I don't want this filthy muck in my mouth.
- Does smoking make me relax? No! It does not! I never smoke sub-consciously – i.e. without thinking
- I only deep breathe healthy, fresh air
- When I see people smoking or drinking, I pity them. I am missing out on nothing!
- "Speak words of life unto thyself." Speak only happy healthy thoughts that negate smoking. Speak happy, healthy facts into existence. (Prov 15:4) (Prov. 18:21)
- Smokers can't see nor understand the flip side of the coin of a non-smoker. Vice versa! It doesn't sink in.

<u>The Catch 22</u>

I will keep repeating the above, (auto suggestion) even while continuing to smoke, drink or the bad habit.

If I can't go "cold turkey" I will continually make small changes & take small steps which will mount up (Kaizen)

If I keep repeating the above, I will eventually give up.

The Key word is "Repetition!" Repeat - even if I don't believe that it will work.

Repeated un-belief becomes belief, and then belief becomes fact.

I memorized all the above and recite it out aloud. I add improvised harmonica solos. It helps me with my breathing. It is part of my live stage act. The healing power of music!

- Consider the Escapism, Freedom, and Happy Home, and Mind, of Jesus. Escape to a Happy Place!
- PRAY! Lord show me the way. Set my feet on Higher Ground. IN the mighty name of Jesus, evil spirit of nicotine and smoking, be gone! Don't come back!
- Every day, I kill off & bury my sins by remorse, confession, and repentance (to think again.) Every-day, I repent (think again) and renew my mind. Every day, I train my mind to only dwell on happy, healthy, righteous, thoughts.

(Rom 6) (Rom 12: 1-2) (Col 3:2) (Phil 4:8)

Check Out these Super- Natural Healings!

The Healings don't always happen but they didn't die out with the Apostles

There are too many to be fraud. Other religions don't have them. They tell me I'm on the right path

The Revival Fellowship: The Last Reformation: Curry Blake: Derek Prince: Spirit Filled Churches:

Music that I write is published on the internet and can be downloaded

There is no obligation, but I appreciate any donations - either to
My PAYPAL Account 003mrh@gmail.com
My Bank Account @ the Adelaide Police Credit Union
BSB 805-005 Acct No. 100233308
By cheque to GPO Box 2404 ADELAIDE Sth Australia 5001

EDUCATION

Salisbury High School (Sth Australia) 1966 to 1970

Winner of a two year Commonwealth Secondary Scholarship (1969 & 1970)

Matriculation (Year 12) (1970)

Studied Science at Adelaide University & Teacher's College (1971 to 1974)

Various Music Courses (over 4 years)

Various Human relations Courses & On the Job Training (over 58 years)

Various Accounting, Salaries, Purchasing, Equal Opportunity, O H & S Courses

Various Sales Courses & On the Job Training

Certificate 3 in German (Adelaide TAFE)

Certificate in Journalism (Adelaide TAFE)

WORK EXPERIENCE

Shop Assistant & Assistant Manager (family and other businesses) 11 years

Class 2 Factory Machinist (12 months)

Public Servant (Admin) (13 years)

Advertising & Printing Sales Rep (12 months)

Literacy Tutor (12 months)

Part time After Hours Music Teacher (at schools & privately) (30 years)
(I had to adapt my music to people of all ages and backgrounds. I have experience with children, seniors, students with disabilities & aboriginals)

I also do live performances with my guitar. I mostly busk, play at Open Mics or perform for small groups of about 20 people.

I write music, have recorded two musical CD's and sold about 500 copies. I get a small, annual, musical royalty payment

I've always had top notch writing skills & was first published in high school (as a 15 year old in 1968).

I've also had my poetry published

I wrote a Budget & Money Saving Booklet and sold about 3000 copies

I got good feed-back with most people telling me that they got their money back – many times over

I also wrote a Healthy Meals Booklet and sold about 5,400 copies.

Again, I got good feed-back with most people telling me that they got their money back – many times over

THE COST

All my life, I tried to produce a diligent work effort, that is in Good Faith, for a fair and reasonable fee.

"The **love of** money is at the root of all evil" (1Tim 6:10) - so I am not money focused.

"A feast causes laughter, wine maketh merry, but money answers all things" (Eccl 10:19)

This doesn't mean to focus on money,
but rather, that everything has a cost.

Usually people who are abused with money, or who have an emotional illness, tend to be reckless spenders. I try not to, but there are times when I waste money.

However, I do have expenses, so I appreciate any donations either to

- My PAYPAL Account hshulten@yahoo.com.au
- My Police Credit Union Acct in Adelaide
  BSB No.805-005 Acct No.5227061
- Or by cheque to
  GPO Box 2404 ADELAIDE Sth Australia 5001